Toby and the Snowflakes

written by Julie Halpern

illustrated by Matthew Cordell

Houghton Mifflin Company
Boston 2004

For Mom, Dad, and Amy, who have always made me feel like I can do anything —J.H.

For Mammy, Pops, Shirley, and Eric —M.C.

For Hannah Rodgers, for making this all possible —J.H. & M.C.

Text copyright © 2004 by Julie Halpern
Illustrations copyright © 2004 by Matthew Cordell

www.houghtonmifflinbooks.com

The text of this book is set in 15-point ITC Garamond 1.
The illustrations are pen and ink with watercolor

ISBN-13: 978-0-618-42004-9
ISBN-10: 0-618-42004-5

Library of Congress Cataloging-in-Publication Data

Halpern, Julie, 1975–
  Toby and the snowflakes / by Julie Halpern ; illustrated by Matthew Cordell.
     p. cm.
  Summary: Lonely after his best friend moves away, Toby finds new playmates in the talking snowflakes that begin to fall.
  ISBN 0-618-42004-5
  [1. Snow—Fiction. 2. Friendship—Fiction. 3. Play—Fiction.] I. Cordell, Matthew, 1975– ill. II. Title.
  PZ7.H1666To 2004
  [E]—dc22
                        2003017728

Printed in Singapore
TWP 10 9 8 7 6 5 4 3 2 1

Toby's best friend moved away yesterday.

All he left behind is his baseball glove that smells like Parmesan cheese.

Toby decides to check the mail. Maybe his best friend has sent him a letter.

Toby walks outside. Snow hasn't fallen in weeks, but the cold keeps the old snow frozen and mucky on the ground.

"Empty," Toby sighs.

Then a snowflake falls.

"Hello," Toby says to the snowflake.

"Hello," the snowflake answers. "My name is Arnold." Another snowflake lands near Arnold. "This is Kevin. Why don't you come and play with us?"

"Okay," says Toby.

Toby stands in the middle of the front lawn. He listens to the voice of each snowflake as it falls to the ground.

Some tell jokes. Others talk about movies they have seen. One snowflake wishes for a warm piece of pecan pie.

The snowflakes fall faster. Piles of snow fluff around Toby's boots.

A snowflake voice calls out, "Come play in us. Be our friend."

Toby steps out into the clean snow. He falls back and lets the piles of
snowflakes catch him. The snow feels warm and comfy around him.

Swish. Swish. "What a delightful snow angel," the snowflakes tell Toby.
"Thanks," he replies.

Toby forms a lumpy clump of snow. When he makes it smooth and round, it reminds him of a baseball.

Toby rolls the snowball on the ground. It grows bigger and bigger.

He makes another.

And another.

"Look at us," gloat the snowflakes. "We make a fine snowman."
"I will call you Dennis," Toby tells the snowman.

Proud and tired, Toby goes inside his house to warm up.

The next morning Toby looks out his window.

The sun shines brightly, and Toby notices that Dennis has sagged to one side. *Maybe he's bored,* Toby thinks.

After bundling up, Toby brings out his best friend's baseball glove and places it on Dennis's twig hand.

"How sporty we look," the snowflakes say.

Toby walks to the mailbox and peeks inside.
"Empty."

He decides to eat a bowl of peaches 'n' cream
oatmeal.

In the afternoon, Toby steps back outside. The sun heats up everything.
Toby watches the piles of snow become smaller and wetter.

He hears the snowflakes call to each other.

"Goodbye, Roger."
"See ya, Sheila."
"Next time around, Yolanda."

"Why is everybody leaving?"

Arnold lands on Toby's mitten. "We all have to go some time."

"But why?" Toby asks.

"Because that is what we do. We snow, we disappear, we come back again.
It is the nature of the snowflake."

Melting snow makes Dennis's twig arm move. *Plop*. The baseball glove falls into the snow.

"Then who will be my friend?"
The snowflakes are too busy melting to answer.
"Hello." Toby hears a new voice from behind him.

It's a boy.

"My name's Gary. I just moved in down the street." Gary picks the baseball glove out of the snow. "Want to come over and play?"

Toby looks at Dennis. He is much smaller and flatter than before.

"Okay," Toby says. "Do you like baseball?"

"Sure," says the new boy. "I have a glove just like this one at home."

"Really?" Toby asks.

"Yep," says Gary. "It smells like cheddar cheese."